His
Name shall be
Fred

FREE

by
Jeffrey Wiebens

To order additional copies of this book, contact:
Xlibris
844-714-8691
www.Xlibris.com
Orders@Xlibris.com

ISBN: Softcover   978-1-6698-4884-4
         EBook   978-1-6698-4883-7

Print information available on the last page

Rev. date: 10/24/2022

His
Name shall be
Fred

Six little puppies that love to play were all in a box that said "free" on display.

1

One by one, they all went away.
Until the littlest pup was alone,
and left to stay. Such a brave
little pup, one would say.

FREE

4

Day by day, alone he stayed, with
no other puppies with which to play.
People would look, then walk away.
Sad and alone in the box he laid.

He onced lived in a box he
shared with his kin. But now
he's been dropped at a shelter
and placed in a pen.

8

Through the bars he saw others
like him. Unloved puppies and
dogs in pens more than ten.

He stayed there for days as others
came and went. All he wanted was
a home and a family he dreamt.
But stuck in his pen with walls
cold and gray, he feared he'd be
alone for the rest of his days.

Until a little girl peeked through
the bars and said "this one
Daddy! I want to name him Fred."
So they took the pup home with
hugs and kisses for his head.

Scared and shaky even when embraced, the littlest pup was still unsure of his fate. But given a new home, new family, and name, the littlest pup began to change. The littlest pup who found a new home started to feel safe, move around and roamed. The littlest pup loved his new home, and showed it with kisses and a tail that wagged on its own.

He cuddled with Mom and Dad
all the same, and played with the
little girl, such wonderful games.
He laid by the window where the sun
warmed his face, and slept in the little
girl's bed, by her feet was his place.

He loved his new home. His new family was great! So he barked a love song to show how happy they made him. The littlest pup found his forever home. Hurray! And his name shall be Fred for the rest of his days.

Printed in the United States
by Baker & Taylor Publisher Services